MARY'S STORY

MARY'S STORY:

A SHORT STORY BASED ON THE BIBLICAL ACCOUNT OF THE BIRTH OF JESUS CHRIST

Baker Family

Hazel Partington and Jody Baker

ISBN: 13-979-8-6880-9793-1

CONTENTS

Forward

This is the first of many offerings from our family to yours. This little story was originally composed by my mother-in-law, (Hazel Partington) when my wife was just a young girl. We have kept it in the family for the last 35 years and believe it is time to share it with you and your family. We hope you enjoy it and are inspired by it.

In Christ,

Jody Baker

To my children:

Since I have spent this Christmas holiday season confined to my bed, I have put together some of my thoughts regarding the events that we refer to as the First Christmas. I decided to write them down and share them with you.

I hope that reading this story will cause you to carefully reread the first two chapters of Matthew and Luke so that you can clearly discern between my imagination, traditions, and biblical fact. It is my hope that in thinking about the possible struggles that Joseph and Mary went through, you will see that God uses the difficulties in the lives of those who trust Him for the good purpose of making our character more like that of His Son. But He can only do that when we lay aside our own expectations and plans and yield to His wonderful will for us.

I hope that you will see in the story that when Mary relied upon God's Word, she had peace and direction for her life. Disappointment and confusion resulted when she relied on her own expectations. I believe that this is true for everyone. Someone wise once said that God does not call the equipped; He equips the called. It is my theory that God knew the hearts of Mary and Joseph - that they desired most of all to do His will - and that is why He chose to use them. But I do not think that they automatically understood and had an easy time of it. No more than we do today.

Mary and Joseph learned to trust God and drew their strength from His Word. So must we. That is my prayer for you. As you read what I have written, I hope you will use it to stimulate your own thoughts about these two godly biblical characters, and consider how their examples might be applied to your own life, and thus encourage you to spend more time in His Word. Love & prayers,

Mama

Christmas 1985

CHAPTER ONE

HER FATHER had taken her hand and said kindly, but firmly, "Mary, angels don't appear nowadays like they did to our ancestors. Do you understand? They don't bring messages from Jehovah to men, much less to a girl!"

Her mother had said nothing, letting her husband deal with it. As they walked away from her, Mary saw her father put his arm around her mother to steady her and Mary knew that she was weeping.

"Joachim," her mother had gasped between sobs, "whatever has happened to our sweet Mary? What are we going to do?"

Joachim guided Anna to their favorite place to sit beneath the almond tree and held her comfortingly. "Lord God, grant us wisdom this hour," he silently prayed.

"Oh, Joachim," she went on, "You know how I have longed for the day when Mary would announce the glad news that she was making me a grandmother. I've dreamed of it so many times! I always thought Joseph would make such a good husband and father. But now this! This is nothing more than a nightmare! Do you think it could be Joseph's baby? I never would have expected that from him, of all people! What will the neighbors say? And what if it isn't Joseph's? What will he do when he finds out? Oh, Joachim! She could be stoned! You don't think they will stone her, do you? Oh, Joachim, I can't bear this! I just can't bear it!" and she began to sob even harder.

He let Anna ramble on as the torrent of painful thoughts and feelings erupted. Joachim knew Anna well. She needed to express all these fears. He knew she wasn't really asking him to answer all her questions; only to listen. He held her gently and let her release all her pent-up emotion. His despair and confusion were no less than that of his wife, but he dealt with them in silence.

"You know," she sniffled, as the sobbing eased up a bit, "I don't think Mary is really even pregnant!" She sat up a little straighter as denial began to mercifully anesthetize her pain. "You know, Mary has been very interested in the prophet Daniel lately. I think that's where she got this idea of an angel. Wasn't that angel even named Gabriel? You see? That proves it! I think she was just out in the hot sun too long today. Don't you think that's it, Joachim? Maybe we should be more watchful of Mary's health. Just because she's such a willing worker, we shouldn't let her overdo. Especially now when she's so excited about her upcoming wedding! Has Joseph finished the house yet, Joachim? Have you asked Nathan to casually wander by there and check it out?

Joachim sat patiently. He could only think of one thing. Time. He needed time to sort all of this out. But what could be done with Mary in the meantime? If she went around telling everyone this story.... What else was it that she had said? An idea was nagging at the back of his brain, but right now he hurt so badly it was hard to think. If only he could still his pounding heart!

"Oh, yes! Elizabeth!" he recalled, "Anna, what was Mary saying about Elizabeth?"

"That's just my point, Joachim! Oh, I'm so glad you see it my way! See? It is all in her mind! Don't you remember when that traveler from the Judean hills came through Nazareth last week and told us about how Zechariah had seen some kind of vision in the Temple? And how now there were all kinds of rumors going around about Elizabeth hiding herself away since he got back home? See how it all fits?" she said triumphantly! "Mary just fantasized that she and poor pitiful Elizabeth are both pregnant. One idea is nearly as preposterous as the other! You see? I'm right! She just dreamed all of this up! Poor child! I'd better get back to the house and comfort her."

"Wait, Anna! Why don't we send Mary to visit Zechariah and Elizabeth? They are godly relatives who truly love Mary. And they live way out in the hill country. Look how long it took for us to hear about Zechariah? Now wouldn't that be a perfect place for

Mary - to rest. And you could find out what the real story is about Elizabeth's reported strange behavior and Zechariah' affliction. The traveler said he can't say a word, remember?" And it will buy us some time, he thought inwardly.

Anna hesitated. She knew that Elizabeth had always been especially fond of Mary. And it was true that if there was anyone they could trust; it would be these two godly relatives. But didn't Mary need her mother if she was going through some kind of strange illness of her thoughts? Yet, it would be interesting, to say the least, to find out the truth about all those rumors about Zechariah and Elizabeth.

"Perhaps you're right," she sighed. "We'd better have her go right away before she has an opportunity to talk to anybody."

"Anyone but Joseph," he declared. "No, Anna" he added as he saw her start to resist. "They are betrothed. I must allow her to let Joseph know that she is going - and why. Joseph is a good man, or at least so I always thought," he commented thoughtfully. "We will simply have to trust that he will do the right thing. Whatever that may be," he added as his voice broke.

They sat together in silence for a while, each drawing strength from the nearness of the other. Then as one they got up and returned to the house. Anna went to tell Mary to prepare for her trip and Joachim set off to make the needed arrangements.

*****

Mary was stunned. How could she tell Joseph?

How could she not tell him? If her own parents did not believe her, how could anyone, even this gentle man she loved, believe such a story? Of course, every Jewish girl dreamed of giving birth to the Messiah - in an abstract, spiritual sort of way - but when it came right down to it, Mary realized in her heart that nobody - not even Joseph - was going to believe that she got pregnant without sinning!

Mary glanced at her wedding dress for what must have been the hundredth time and sighed audibly. This should be such a time of excitement and anticipation! Betrothed to such a wonderful man!

But now.... She sighed again.

"Guide me, Lord, and give me the strength to do whatever You would have me say and do," she prayed.

She sighed again. She wished Joseph would come soon so she could get this over with.

*****

As Joseph headed for Mary's home, he hummed to himself. An hour ago, he was so exhausted from spending every spare moment building the house that he could hardly move a muscle. Now as the home of Mary's parents came into view, his step was so light he could hardly maintain his dignity and keep from running. How he loved his cherished little bride!

He could hardly wait to take her home to this house he was building for her. Just today he had finished the roof. Soon he would begin work on the table where they would recline together and share their meals and their thoughts after a busy day. He had been saving an especially beautiful piece of precious oak for this project for a long time and could hardly wait to begin working on it. How her eyes would shine when she saw what he had made for her. Joseph had decided that everything would be just perfect before he brought her to their new home, even though he hated waiting another moment. He ached to hold her and marveled at the thought that soon she would be his and his alone for the rest of their lives!

He slowed his pace just long enough to stoop down and pick a little daisy blooming along the path. How much she was like this fragile flower, so pure and simple in its beauty. He thanked His Creator once again for the privilege of knowing and loving her.

*****

All the weariness had returned to Joseph's tired body - and more. He felt like he could hardly lift one foot in front of the other as he trudged back down the path, he had so recently hurried up to see his bride-to-be. It seemed like it had been years, not minutes ago. It was an entirely different world now. He didn't notice the wildflowers along the path this time. Everything looked bleak and dark.

Joseph felt like he was being pulled down into the depths of disappointment and despair. How could this be? How could he have been so wrong about Mary? Pregnant? He never would have dreamed that she wasn't trustworthy. What was he supposed to do now? What about the house and all the work he had put into it? And in the depths of his grief, he allowed his mind to dwell on the little nearly irrelevant things until they consumed his thoughts lest he be forced to face a bigger issue so dark and monstrous that it might swallow him up into it if he tried to face it too quickly.

"Maybe I'll use that piece of oak for something else," he said aloud. And the sound of his own voice startled him. Without Mary any old piece of wood for his table would do just as well.

*****

It was many miles to the hill country and Mary had a great deal of time to think as she traveled along. She reflected on the conversation she'd had with her parents and the bitter disappointment and shock she had felt when they hadn't believed her. Now they were further rejecting her by sending her away. She had wanted to resist them, but Mary had been taught that God works and protects through the lines of authority He has established, so she knew that she must obey them even though they clearly did not understand. At least she liked the idea of the visit to her older relatives in the hill country. If she had to be sent someplace, she was glad it was there. Mary tried to imagine what it would be like to see Elizabeth and be the one to tell her the astounding news that they were both going to have sons! And that an angel had told her about Elizabeth's pregnancy! And imagine the look on Elizabeth's face to hear that she was pregnant herself even now.

And how it had all happened!

Then she began to wonder if Zechariah and Elizabeth would believe her when obviously no one else had. She puzzled over the rumors about Zechariah' vision in the Temple. Did he see Gabriel, too? No, she didn't think so. After all, Zechariah was afflicted from that encounter, whatever it was. They said he couldn't hear or speak a word. Certainly nothing like that had happened to her when she had spoken to Gabriel. No, his vision must have been something entirely different. Maybe, though, having had an extraordinary spiritual experience would somehow make him more likely to believe her. She certainly hoped so.

It would be good to be with her own dear relative who was going through a pregnancy, too. What a blessing it would be to have another woman she loved so dearly to share this special time with and help her adjust to all the physical and emotional changes she had heard are associated with pregnancy. But then, perhaps her pregnancy with the Messiah wouldn't be like that of other women.

She was thanking God that He allowed her to get to see Elizabeth when it occurred to her that He had provided just what she would need through her parents even though their motives for sending her were all wrong.

"Help me to trust in Your provision," she prayed.

Yet as the long day wore into evening and Mary struggled to keep up the pace, she gradually forgot about how excited she had been about seeing her relatives. She began to dread their meeting. What could she say to them? They would probably see her as just a foolish young girl. Yet, on the other hand, she was anxious for the journey to end. She felt so fatigued. Had her body ever felt this tired before? It worried her.

Mary's eyes caught sight of a clump of daisies growing near the roadside. At the sight of them her troubled thoughts turned toward Joseph. Was it only last night that he had so thoughtfully handed her a similar token of his love? Right after that, she had told him. Now everything was different.

Yet she knew that she had made the right choice. She would serve God however He asked, even if that meant giving up her beloved Joseph. She wondered, though, if the pain would ever go away. Would she ever be able to forget the look of agony and disbelief on his face when she told him? The anguish she had seen in his eyes haunted her. She was glad they had parted quickly.

His silence was so painful. She had so desperately hoped that she might somehow find a way to tell him so that he could understand and share the joyful secret brought by the messenger from God. Yet she realized how incredible her story must have sounded. What a shock it must have been to dear Joseph. His kind, loving heart must be terribly wounded. She prayed for him as she walked along.

*****

The third day of her journey was even more confusing and difficult for Mary. The excitement and enthusiasm had all drained away and she felt weary and discouraged. Doubts assailed her from every direction. Could all this really have happened? Yes, her greatest desire in life was to be of service to God, but how could that mean He would choose her to bear the Messiah? It didn't make any sense. She was just a simple girl from tiny Nazareth. There were certainly many other Jewish girls who were more talented and intelligent than she. How could she ever think she could handle such a task, anyway?

Mary didn't doubt that God could accomplish whatever He desired, even in her. But was she wrong about hearing Him in the first place? How could it be? If God had really given her the assignment of bearing the Messiah, then surely, He would have also convinced all those who loved her that she was telling the truth, wouldn't He?

Maybe her mother had been right. Maybe she had worked out in the sun too long and this was the beginning of some strange illness. But could any illness cause her to feel the awe she had felt in Gabriel's presence? Well, how could she know what illnesses could do? She was only a girl. One thing she did know for sure, she certainly felt sick this morning!

*****

In the following days Joseph grieved deeply. He mourned the loss of the Mary he thought he had known. He mourned the loss of all the plans and dreams and expectations for their marriage he had cherished. He felt numb and confused. What was he to do? What had gone wrong? How could she have let him down like this? Why couldn't she have at least been honest with him? He had thought they had such open communication. Yet even when she had confessed her pregnancy to him, she hadn't leveled with him. Instead she had told him some outrageous story about an angel. He was miserable.

As Joseph worked in his carpenter's shop on a neighbor's plow, he tried to sort things out. Nothing made any sense to him. One minute he was angry with Mary for letting him down and the next he was angry at himself for being so gullible that he could be so completely fooled by her. What troubled him the most, however, were the times when he realized that he was very angry at God. He sincerely wanted to do the will of God and had been so sure that he was in God's will in taking Mary to be his wife. Why did God permit him to be so wrong about that? Didn't He even care? These were the questions that agonized him the most.

*****

One day Joseph caught himself staring at a handful of nails he was holding. Just staring at them. What was so significant about nails? How long had he been standing there staring at those nails in his hand? He sighed as he thought once more that there didn't seem to be any answers for him. He admitted to himself that he still loved Mary very deeply. His heart ached when he recalled the pain on her sweet face when he could not believe her story about the angel's message and the subsequent manner of conception. But how could any thinking man believe such a tale?

"Oh God," his heart cried out. "What would You have me do?" He thought about the story he had heard recently in his shop about the girl from a nearby town who had been judged for committing adultery. She had been cruelly stoned to her death. He just couldn't let that happen to Mary. But what was he to do? He couldn't bring home a wife and spend the rest of his life in a marriage built on a foundation of deception and sin, could he?

He thought about the ancient prophet Hosea and wondered what it must have been like for him. But Joseph knew that he was no prophet. God had never spoken to him like He did to the prophets of old. No, God would not want him to begin his marriage on such a foundation.

Yet he couldn't bear the thought of shaming Mary and exposing her to public ridicule. Somehow, he must find a way to protect her from that and quietly sign the necessary legal papers without a public judgment. Perhaps his friend Silas would know how he should go about this. Yet even as the thought occurred to him, Joseph realized that he was not ready to share this painful information even with his closest friend.

*****

As the days slowly passed, Joseph was still no closer to a solution. Yet, he found that more and more he was drawing his strength from the Scriptures he had learned as a boy in the synagogue. Over and over he repeated the prayer of David:

Hear, O Lord, and answer me for I am poor and needy.

Guard my life, for I am devoted to you.

You are my God; save your servant who trusts in you.

Have mercy on me, O Lord, for I call to you all day long.

Bring joy to your servant, for to you O Lord I lift up my soul.

You are forgiving and good, O Lord, abounding in love to all who call to you. Hear my prayer, O Lord;

Listen to my cry for mercy.

In the day of my trouble I will call to you for you will answer me. Among the gods there is none like you O Lord; No deeds can compare with yours.

All the nations you have made will come and worship before you O Lord; They will bring glory to your name.

For you are great and do marvelous deeds; You alone are God.

Teach me your way, O Lord, and I will walk in your truth; Give me an undivided heart, that I may fear your name.

I will praise you, O Lord my God, with all my heart;

I will glorify your name forever,

For great is your love toward me;

You have delivered me from the grave.

The arrogant are attacking me, O God; a band of ruthless men seeks my life – men without regard for you.

But you, O Lord, are a compassionate and gracious God, slow to anger, abounding in love and faithfulness.

Turn to me and have mercy on me;

Grant your strength to your servant and save the son of your maidservant.

Give me a sign of your goodness, that my enemies may see it and be put to shame, for you O Lord, have helped and comforted me.

(Psalm 86)

As the words of the ancient psalm penetrated Joseph's very being, he identified with his famous ancestor in a way he had never known before. Clearly David's dependence was fully on God and that must also be true for him. Like David, Joseph began to long for an undivided heart. His anger at God diminished and his devotion deepened as he continued to struggle to find God's solution for his difficult circumstances.

*****

The last day of her journey was the worst for Mary. The weather was disagreeable, and her mood was as dismal as the grey skies above her. She could feel the anxiety mounting. She chided herself for ever attempting to make the trip, forgetting that she was doing it in obedience to her father. She thought about the traveler's words about how Zechariah was unable to hear or speak and how Elizabeth had been keeping completely to herself. It sounded to her like they had enough problems already without adding hers. What right did she have to intrude?

There was no one to be seen as she neared the house. A sense of humiliation and confusion began to rise in Mary's throat. She felt sick and fatigued and totally unable to handle the situation. But there was no turning back. She hesitantly approached, summoned her last ounce of courage, and called out to Elizabeth.

Instead of the reserved response that she had anticipated, Mary was astounded to hear Elizabeth return her salutation with a shout of joy and praise to God for Mary's unborn son!

For Mary it was like the burst of a dam. All the pain and worries and doubts and fears were swept away at Elizabeth's unexpected greeting. All was replaced with unspeakable joy!

Elizabeth knew! It was all true! Their mingled joy multiplied in wave after wave of praise extolling God's goodness, His mercy, His mighty power, and for all He was about to accomplish!

Zechariah silently watched the two enraptured women and sensed with a certainty deeper than his own thoughts, that at this moment the angel's words had been fulfilled and his son had been filled with the Holy Spirit right there in his mother's womb. The ecstasy on Elizabeth's face was unmistakable and even though he could not hear her words, he knew that she was lifting her voice in praise to God and his heart joined in their rejoicing.

Mary was overwhelmed with a sense of God's lovingkindness towards her. How much it meant to her to hear another human voice confirming the angel's message. How God had blessed her by bringing her here!

*****

The bonds between the two pregnant women grew deeper and deeper as the godly old lady mentored the willing young girl. In the weeks that passed they spent many delightful hours together pondering the inscrutable mysteries God was revealing through their lives. They marveled at what it all might mean.

The old priest understood that God was using his wife as His instrument to equip Mary for the task He had given her. In his silence Zechariah interceded for the two women and praised God for all that He was doing. His muteness gave him plenty of undisturbed time to contemplate how God would have him train his son so that he would be prepared for his role in making the people ready to receive Mary's son, the coming Messiah.

It had troubled Mary's kind heart that Zechariah had been afflicted when he had been given his part of the wonderful news. One day she decided to see if he had any idea why that had happened to him, but not to her. She wrote her question on the wax-covered tablet that they used to communicate with him.

“I didn't believe him. You only asked how it would be accomplished," he immediately scratched back with his little wooden stylus.

"Will you ever get better?" she questioned.

Zechariah shrugged. "That timing must be left in the hands of the Lord God," was his written reply.

Elizabeth helped Mary work through her bitterness over being misunderstood and abandoned by those she loved. She patiently guided her into a clearer understanding that it was to be left to the work of the Holy Spirit to change hearts. Mary learned to leave those she loved in God's capable hands and trust Him with the situation. She experienced the healing and freedom of allowing God to complete the work of forgiveness by asking Him to take back any ground she had relinquished to evil in her disappointment and bitterness.

Gradually, under the godly woman's counsel, Mary began to mature and grow in her love for the will of God. The faith of her older relative strengthened Mary's faith and her love for God deepened in a way she previously could not have known. She had made her choice to serve God above all others -even herself - and struggled to know how to live out that choice.

Finally, the day came when Mary had to leave the home of Zechariah. Elizabeth would be delivering soon, and it would not be acceptable for Mary to be there at the birth. Mary left the home of Zechariah and Elizabeth knowing that the two would be faithfully interceding for her. She had arrived willing, but unequipped, to meet the task before her. Now, with God's help, she was ready.

Baker Family

CHAPTER TWO

JOSEPH had half-heartedly continued to work on his house to avoid the inevitable questions that would come if the neighbors saw him abandoning his project at the time of Mary's sudden absence. Everything in the house was nearly finished now. All his wonderful plans for special little details to delight Mary were forgotten.

Now it was just a house. It was certainly not the very special place he had dreamed of for his precious little bride. Anyone could live here now. Sometimes he wondered who might be living there a year from now. Somehow, he didn't think he would be there.

It did not seem important anymore. Joseph found his peace in the Lord now. He lay on his mat and as he drifted off to sleep, his thoughts turned once again to the psalm of his ancestor:

Teach me your way, O Lord, and I will walk in your truth; Give me an undivided heart, that I may fear your name.

I will praise you, O Lord my God, with all my heart;

I will glorify your name forever,

For great is your love toward me;

You have delivered me from the grave.

Yes, it certainly had felt like the depths of the grave that night he had last seen Mary nearly three months ago. He wondered at the peace he now knew. It was beyond his understanding, but his heart sang out in grateful praise to his God. It had definitely been a time of brokenness for him. He could unquestionably see that something new had crystallized in his character as he had struggled and prayed and sought an undivided heart, as his ancestor David had prayed for so long ago. He knew now that the most important thing in his life was his desire to know and do the will of God.

Everything else had become secondary.

He still did not know just how he would ever go about the matter of divorcing Mary quietly, but his peace was in knowing that God was at the center of his life and he would wait and let God show him how to do it. As he waited, he continued to pray for Mary and he drifted off to sleep. As he slept, he had an astounding dream:

"Son of David...." The angel began, as at last Joseph's wait came to an end! Now he knew just what God wanted him to do and he could barely wait for morning light to obey.

*****

Joachim headed for the field to see if his flax was ready for harvest. It was still a little early, but he had decided he might as well get up and start the day. He couldn't sleep anyway. Joachim's heart was heavy as he walked over the ground still wet with dew. Mary's return had filled him with ambivalence. On the one hand, he had to admit he had missed her terribly and was glad to see her, but on the other hand, he found he felt betrayed and very angry. Instead of returning restored and cured of what he had desperately hoped might somehow be a passing illness, she had come back more confident and purposeful. Worst of all, Anna assured him that now there could be no question. Mary was pregnant. It was all so confusing. What should he do now? What could he do?

As he looked up, the sight he dreaded most met his eyes. In the distance he could see the unmistakable figure of Joseph heading directly toward him. Once, he thought bitterly, it was a sight that gave him great joy. He and Anna had been so pleased with this betrothal. They had thought that Joseph was such a godly, dependable man and would make a wonderful husband and father. But if it wasn't Joseph who had done this to his daughter, then who could it be? How many times in the past three months had he and Anna asked each other that question? Yet, Joseph had appeared to be as shocked and hurt as they. It just didn't make any sense.

Now, he supposed, Joseph had heard that Mary was back, and he was on his way there to settle this matter once and for all. The best he could hope for would be that Joseph would ask for a letter of divorcement that the four of them could agree on privately.

When Mary had first left, they had feared that in his hurt and anger Joseph would shame her publicly or even see to it that she was stoned. He had the right. They had been grateful that he had kept the matter to himself.

Joachim sighed and pretended to be so busy that he didn’t notice Joseph's approach. It gave him time to compose himself.

Joseph came up to him and addressed him respectfully.

"Joachim, with your permission, I would like to take Mary into my home today."

Joachim's head shot up. Had he heard Joseph correctly? Was he now going to marry her anyway? Or did that mean that Joseph had been the guilty party and had taken all this time to own up to it? If he had only done this three months ago, maybe they could have avoided all the gossip and fuss. It certainly was too late for that now! Anger coursed through Joachim's veins.

He didn't understand all this and felt powerless to do anything about it.

"I'll go get her," he said abruptly, and started for the house. Rude or not, he'd had enough and wanted to see the end of the matter as fast as possible. Then maybe he and Anna could get on with their own lives. These two had already caused them enough pain.

*****

There would be no lovely wedding, no need for her beautiful dress, so it didn't take Mary long to gather up her few things.

Joseph had followed Joachim back to the house - at a judicious distance - and waited patiently under the almond tree for Mary to appear. As she approached, he went up to her and took her bundle from her. She kept her gaze on the ground, not knowing what to expect.

"Mary," he said. His voice was low and full of anguish. "Can you forgive me for not believing you?" Her eyes cautiously sought his, searching to see what she hoped beyond hope was still there. Yes! The look of love on his face was even stronger than she had ever seen it before. Her heart silently sang out her praises to God, as he continued to implore her for forgiveness. As she returned his gaze, he realized that he did not need to ask again. All had been restored.

Joseph could hardly get out the words fast enough as he told her about his dream and the encounter with the angel. His relief at knowing the truth had made his heart so light that he felt like dancing!

"And Mary," he continued, "the angel said we must name the child Jesus!" Mary gasped! Now she knew without a shadow of a doubt that this had been no ordinary dream - no human subconscious attempt to solve a difficult dilemma. The name! God had given it to both of them! As the child's legal father, Joseph would be the one to name the child. Now it was abundantly clear to Mary that God had ordained Joseph to be the earthly father of the child she carried.

A deep sense of unity and peace enveloped Joseph and Mary as they moved together into the center of God's will for their lives. They hurried down the path together, heading for their new home.

CHAPTER THREE

MARY laughed at herself as she moved clumsily across the floor. I waddle like mother's old goose, she thought. A wave of loneliness so real that it felt like physical pain engulfed her.

How she longed to be sharing these times with her family and friends. Yet, no one came to see her. She and Joseph were completely isolated.

"Thank You for providing my wonderful Joseph," she prayed aloud. What would have become of her if he had continued to reject her, too? She still desired to serve God as He directed, but that didn't mean she didn't long for at least one female friend to share with now. How grateful she was that God had provided Elizabeth in those first months. How she had been blessed in those times. Yes, God was faithful, she reminded herself. He would provide all that she needed. She would accept whatever came from His hand.

"Lord God," she prayed. "Give me a grateful heart. And help me to keep trusting You." As Mary prayed her hands were busy with the strips of cloth she was folding that Elizabeth had given her. Just rags, really, but they were scrubbed as clean as they could possibly be. I probably won't need them to swaddle the baby with, anyway, she thought. Surely God will provide something better for His Son.

Her thoughts turned once again as they often did these days to dreaming about the birth of her baby. She was convinced that this would be no ordinary birth.

"After all," she had reasoned to Joseph, "the conception was miraculous, so the birth might be too." And she had shared some of her ideas with him about how it might happen. Perhaps they would wake up one morning and he would be lying there sleeping contentedly between them on their mat. Or would he suddenly just appear in her arms? Her favorite scenario included the angel. After all, he had announced the coming birth. Perhaps he would be there to present the baby to them in some glorious way!

Joseph had not been so sure that Mary was correct about a miraculous birth and had borne the humiliation of going to Anna and pleading with her to help Mary when the time came. It was humbling, but he had felt much better after he had extracted a hesitant promise from her mother to attend the birth. Mary could see that Joseph was visibly relieved to know that her mother would be there.

That was all right with her. Dear Joseph was only trying to look out for her. But he would see. She was glad her mother would be there. Then she would see for herself that this was a miraculous baby. Maybe her mother would even get to talk to the angel! Then her lonely days would be over. Then everyone would not only believe her but would support and love her again. Not that she wanted to be praised; Mary was far too humble for that. But it would be so nice to be past this painful time of rejection and loneliness and be loved and accepted by family and friends again.

Just as she was finishing her task, Joseph came bursting into their little home. The alarm on his face frightened her.

"Mary, you'll never believe what the Romans just announced in the marketplace! More taxes! A census! We must go to Bethlehem to register in the city of my ancestors! Right away!"

"But we are Jews. We belong to God, not to the Romans! Why should we have to submit to the tax laws of these pagan overlords?" she resisted.

"Besides, Joseph, how could we possibly go all the way to Bethlehem? It's nearly my time!"

"I know, dear one, but the Romans have no regard for such things as births. Life is of little value to them. We have no choice. We must go."

"This is terrible, Joseph!" Mary wept. How could God allow such a thing? But she knew they had no choice. One did not argue with the mighty Roman government - and live. She began to pack the supplies they would need for their journey. "Maybe I'd better pack these, too, just in case," she sighed as her eyes rested on the strips of cloth she had been folding.

*****

The journey to Bethlehem was long and arduous. As Joseph walked along, he thought about his upcoming role as father of his adopted son. He had often enviously watched his friend Silas and young Matthew and marveled at how close they had become. Silas was the smith who lived nearby. Joseph and Silas often worked together to combine their skills in making and repairing farm implements for their customers. He still remembered the day when Silas had told him about his plans to marry the young widow Miriam who already had a little son named Matthew. At the time Joseph had wondered if he could ever love a child someone else had fathered as much as one of his own. Now the question seemed so ridiculous!

Could any birthfather ever have been more excited about the birth of his child? Joseph felt a thrill go through him at the thought of becoming a father. And what a fortunate father he was!

He even knew that this child would be a son before he was born!

"Jesus!" he whispered as he imagined himself calling to his little son. He treasured the thoughts as they trudged along. "Hear my prayer, O Lord," he murmured. "And grant me the wisdom and courage I'll need to be a good father to Jesus."

*****

It had been their fourth day out on the dusty road and Mary hadn't had a very good night. It had become increasingly difficult to find a comfortable position lately, but last night had been the worst. Her back really hurt and she had felt restless all night.

The surprising thing was that this morning she felt bursting with energy!

"I must just be excited about seeing Jerusalem today," she told Joseph. Their destination was just a few miles south of the great city. She could hardly wait for that first glimpse of the Temple rising majestically like a shining white mountain. "Oh Joseph, maybe Jesus will be born in one of the palaces of Jerusalem," she enthused.

"Mary," he said gently, "how would we ever get into a palace?"

"But remember what the angel said?" she returned. "'With God nothing is impossible!'"

"And do you really think that you and I would be comfortable in a palace? We wouldn't even know how to act," he chided as he grinned at her affectionately. "Besides, Mary," he continued more seriously now. "I've been thinking a lot about the prophet Micah this morning. Remember how we studied the Scriptures to see what they had prophesied about the Messiah?"

"Yes, Joseph," she responded eagerly. Mary loved it when her husband discussed the Scriptures with her, especially the ones that spoke about the coming Christ.

"Remember how we had decided that his reference to the city of David would somehow be fulfilled because our families were originally from Bethlehem? Now I am wondering if God meant it literally, Mary. I don't know where or how, but I think maybe God was saying that His Son – our son – (he added with such awe at the thought that his voice cracked), will actually be born right there in the town of Bethlehem."

Mary thought about his words for a long time. Where in Bethlehem would they find a place good enough for the Messiah to be born? It was fun to think about. Her favorite story of all their ancestors was that of another Joseph born long ago. Hadn't he been sold by his brothers into slavery? Yet by trusting God he had become second in command of the whole nation of Egypt! Surely, the Messiah would be even greater than Joseph or David. "Joseph," she exclaimed, as another thought struck her. "Do you remember what Joseph said to his brothers?"

At first Joseph just looked bewildered. He had been deep in thought. Her behavior this morning troubled him. He wasn't sure exactly what it was all about, but he vaguely recalled the womenfolk talking about a spurt of energy that often comes sometime before a woman gives birth. He wished he knew more. Did that mean soon or in several days? He was not sure. He had been thinking so hard about how he might find a safe place for her in Bethlehem for the next few days that he didn't even know how long she had been speaking.

"You meant it for evil, but God meant it for good," she quoted. Joseph was relieved. Now he knew whom she was talking about. Not long ago they had studied the story of his ancient namesake together. Oh, that he would be able to patiently trust in God like that Joseph had!

"You know," Mary continued. "I think that is just like our situation with the Romans. You see? They meant this census for evil. We are certainly taxed to death already. But God meant it for good. Now I think I'm beginning to see, Joseph. He is using this census to send us to Bethlehem – the City of David – where the Christ is to be born. We just didn't get it."

"Oh Joseph!" she exclaimed, as yet another thought overwhelmed her, "Isn't it incredible to think that the Lord God is so powerful that He can even tell the mighty Roman Empire what to do?" After some moments of thoughtful silence, Mary added in an incredulous voice, "Do you think when the prophet Isaiah said that the Christ would be a light for the Gentiles, he meant even the Romans?!"

As the day passed Mary became increasingly aware that the walking seemed to be having an effect on her womb. Sometimes it would feel so strange. Her belly would get as hard as a rock. She and Joseph laughed about it and she chatted with him again about how special and extraordinary this birthing would be. Mary did not notice the worry lines creasing his brow. Joseph silently prayed his favorite psalm as he walked along:

Have mercy on me, O Lord, for I call to you all day long....

How would they ever find a decent place to stay when they reached Bethlehem? Mary seemed unaware of how many other travelers had hurried past them as he tried to keep a pace that she could handle with her cumbersome body so heavy with child. But Joseph noticed and fretted about how late in the day they would arrive in a town that must already be teeming with others who were also descendants of David.

They could hear the tumult coming out of the town before they even reached their destination. Boisterous merchants and travelers were everywhere. It was so strange to be amid the noise and confusion. It seemed threatening and frightening to the gentle couple accustomed to the more rustic lifestyle of quiet Nazareth.

***

CHAPTER FOUR

MARTHA moved to the back doorway to catch a breath of fresh air and pause for just a moment in the midst of her busy preparations for all her guests. So many to feed! Her eye caught sight of yet another couple coming up the dusty path toward their inn. They had had to turn people away for the last few hours now.

"Why do they still come?" she thought irrationally. She had never been so overwhelmed in her entire life.

As they moved toward her, Martha could not pull her gaze away from the face of the young girl. She noticed the way the girl walked as her husband tenderly supported her. She didn't miss the sudden change of expression as the girl's hand moved quickly to her swollen belly. There was no doubt in Martha's mind. She had borne five children herself and she knew instantly what was happening. Her heart went out to the sweet-faced young girl. Obviously, this would be her first. And at such a time!

"Samuel!" she called to her youngest who was trying to help her. "Watch this bread for me until I get back. I must have a word with your father." And she hurried off to find her busy husband.

"Martha, you know we are more than filled to overflowing now," he protested when she had made her plea. "What would you have me do? Even our own rooms were filled long ago! It's impossible!"

As Martha returned to her duties, she smiled to herself. Joshua was a kind man. She knew he would see to her request in the best way that he could.

Just as the couple reached the inn, Samuel appeared at his father's side. Joshua knew instantly that Martha had sent him to discover how he had handled her request. A good woman, his wife, but when she set her mind to something....

"Samuel," he addressed his son, "You'd better go feed the stock now." Perhaps if he could get rid of Samuel, Martha would be too busy to remember the errand she had sent him on. He couldn't help noticing that the girl leaned heavily against the side of the inn as her husband left her to approach him. He pictured a baby being born right there in the middle of his courtyard. That would certainly not make a very restful night for his many weary travelers. But what could he do?

"Already did!" Samuel was saying, interrupting his father's thoughts. "I even cleaned out Old Methuselah's stall," he added proudly. The father smiled at his son.

He knew that the crowds were hard on this his most sensitive child. He had found something useful to do while he escaped to the serenity of the stable for a break. He was a blessed man to have such a fine family.

"Thank You, Lord for the blessings of my family. Guide my steps." He prayed automatically as he was accustomed to doing. The memory of the day when Samuel was born flashed through his mind unexpectedly and the thought refreshed him from all the worries of the frantic day. Now as he looked into the face of the weary man approaching him, an idea occurred to him.

"Please, sir," Joseph began. "Have you any place where we could spend the night? My wife...."

"Samuel," Joshua interrupted. "Take these tired travelers to Methuselah's stall and bring him out to be tied with the donkeys of the other guests."

"Sir," he said as he turned back to Joseph, "I'm sorry, but that is the best I can do." He turned abruptly to speak with one of the servants waiting nearby for his next orders.

"Follow me!" said young Samuel and he headed for the old donkey's stall.

"Ooooh!" Mary gasped, as another contraction slammed against her body. She stopped and felt Joseph's strong arm steady her. In barely a minute it had passed. She smiled considerately into Samuel's alarmed face.

"I'm okay now," she said softly. He looked flustered and waited for Joseph to tell him what to do. Joseph motioned for him to lead on.

Silent the rest of the way, Samuel showed them the freshly cleaned stall and led the old donkey out. Almost immediately he was back, anxious to help Joseph fix a comfortable pile of straw for Mary.

"Jehovah Jireh!" Mary breathed as she sank down on the soft straw. "Thank you, Lord, for providing a tranquil place to rest in the midst of all this clamorous place. I would not trade the serenity of this cozy nest for any palace in the world!" She sighed contentedly as she snuggled down into the straw and almost immediately fell into an exhausted sleep.

Now that he had Joseph's attention, Samuel was full of questions.

"My mother says that you are going to have a baby soon. Where will you put it?"

Joseph certainly wasn't thinking about that yet, and he looked around distractedly.

"How about Old Methuselah's manger?" Samuel suggested. "It is just the right size for a little baby. I will fill it with the best straw I can find!"

Joseph smiled at Samuel's enthusiasm. "Sure. That will be just fine," he responded - more to appease the excited little lad than anything. He was too tired to be thinking of things that could wait until morning, but he didn't want to be unkind to the only one in the city trying to give them aid - even if he was only a child. Besides, he hoped that if the solution satisfied the boy, he would soon leave, and Joseph could join Mary in some much-needed rest. He was relieved to see Mary sleeping so peacefully. In the morning he would make better arrangements and locate a midwife to be ready just in case Mary's ideas were wrong about the miraculous birth.

*****

"Joseph!!" She gasped suddenly as she bolted up out of her sleep. At that moment Mary knew without a doubt that she had been dead wrong about how this baby would be birthed! It was coming and it was coming now! There was no time to find a midwife--no time for anything!

"Lord God!" she pleaded, "Help me! Help Joseph know what to do! "And she tried to focus her mind on the psalm they so often had recited together:

Hear, O Lord, and answer me for I am poor and needy.

Guard my life, for I am devoted to you.

You are my God; save your servant who trusts in you.

*****

Joseph left a light burning dimly so he could gaze at his beautiful sleeping wife and the tiny infant, whom she had so lovingly swaddled in the cloths she had brought before she placed him in the manger Samuel had prepared. He couldn't even consider trying to sleep. His body felt like it was vibrating with excitement and energy. He was bursting with a desire to share his good news with somebody - anybody! He wished he could shout it from the housetops. But who would care? Who would even listen?

No, his place was here watching over his dear Mary and their newborn son. His heart swelled at the thought of them. "Lord God," he prayed, "Show me how to be a good husband to Mary and father to Your Son." As he prayed for strength and wisdom for himself, he prayed for all new fathers who must, like him, also feel totally inadequate to handle the sacred responsibility of parenting a child. He wondered if it were even possible to tire of watching the tiny newborn face, now so relaxed in sleep in his makeshift cradle. Preoccupied with his thoughts, he hardly noticed that the muted sounds from the busy town were getting louder.

There was the sound of running feet and a voice very nearby shouted, "There's a light! It's got to be the one!" Before he realized what was happening, several excited men burst into the tiny, cramped stall. Joseph was on his feet in an instant, ready to protect his two precious charges. But the look of reverent awe on the faces of these rough outdoorsmen was so astounding that he sat back down quickly. Mary had awakened at the disturbance and he put his arm around her and supported her as they gazed in silent astonishment as the shepherds prostrated themselves before the tiny infant and worshipped Him.

After they got up, they began to tell their thrilling story, interrupting each other in their excitement. Mary's eyes widened in wonder. So, the angel had played a part in the birth after all! Not as she had expected, but to share the wonderful news with these humble shepherds.

She listened quietly, trying to take it all in so she could savor the memory of every detail in the days ahead. She was glad now that she had experienced a natural birth. Looking back on those moments, she knew she would always treasure the sense of God's nearness she had felt as she toiled to bear her child. She was learning that she must set aside her own expectations of how things would be and just trust and obey as God directed. His ways were truly beyond what her mind could conceive.

Mary recalled what the prophet Isaiah had said when he had been talking about the Messiah. It made so much sense to her now:

"'For my thoughts are not your thoughts, neither are your ways my ways,' declares the Lord."

"Help me Lord, to learn to love Your ways," she prayed. "Joseph," she murmured, as she eased herself back down into the soft straw, "wasn't our ancestor David once a shepherd in those same fields?" And Mary drifted into a peaceful sleep.

*****

Early the next morning Samuel timidly peeked into the stall. Joseph put his finger to his lips and motioned for him to come closer and peer into the manger. Samuel's eyes filled with wonder as he discovered the tiny baby in the manger, he had so carefully prepared. Joseph got up and offered to help Samuel with his morning chores. Samuel chattered animatedly about all the guests staying at the inn, completely forgetting that Mary was still asleep. Joseph started to shush him, then caught Mary's eye and knew that she had awakened and was enjoying listening to the little boy sharing his experiences with him. His heart thrilled at the knowledge that someday soon their own little boy would be doing this. Every now and then he would send Mary a secret smile behind Samuel's back until the lad left them.

Presently Samuel was back with some curds. "I told my mother about the baby and she sent some of these for you," he said and shyly handed them to Mary, his eyes glued to the baby in her arms.

"Would you like to hold him, Samuel?" she asked graciously. Samuel looked down at the straw and shuffled his feet. He wasn't sure he was quite ready for that.

"I noticed that your father's wooden cart is in need of repair," Joseph interjected to ease the boy's discomfort. "I am a carpenter and would be happy to fix it for him in exchange for his kindness. Do you think you could find me some tools if he would like to have me do that?"

"Sure!" Samuel responded. "My uncle was a carpenter here in Bethlehem, but he has been badly injured and had to go and stay with my cousins. When all the travelers from the census leave, his shop and the room in back of it where he lives will be empty. Maybe you could stay there for a while and help out. A lot of people in Bethlehem would be overjoyed to hear there's another carpenter in town. Our only other carpenter is old Ebenezer and he is just too old to keep up with all the work. He'd be the happiest one of all to have you stay. His son Jacob tries, but he doesn't like the work and he's not good at it. I'll ask my father about it the first chance I get!" Joseph and Mary smiled at each other as the young boy hurried off on his new errand

*****

A short time later Samuel burst into the stall.

"Joseph! Joseph! You won't believe what they are saying about our baby!" He stopped suddenly and looked very embarrassed. He hadn't intended to reveal to them that he had been referring to their son as "our" baby. But deep inside he felt very much like this baby belonged to him, too. He didn't understand it; he didn't even try. But with a child's heart he sensed that it was somehow true.

He looked out of the corner of his eye to see how Joseph had reacted to the slip of his tongue, but Joseph's smile was warm and encouraging.

"What are they saying, Samuel?" he invited.

"Everyone is saying that last night some shepherds were all over town telling everybody that angels appeared in the sky. And even more than that! They said that the angels told them to look for a baby in swaddling cloths in a manger because he was the promised Messiah! And they told everybody that they found him here! What does it all mean, Joseph?"

Patiently they told Samuel their story and how the angel had appeared to each of them. He listened intently and with the faith of a child, he quietly slipped to his knees before the baby and reverently worshipped the tiny Christ.

CHAPTER FIVE

DURING HER TIME OF SEPARATION, Mary spent a great deal of time thinking about all that had occurred. She thanked God daily for His provision of the little room off the carpenter shop. As the end of the forty days drew near, they made their plans to travel the few miles to Jerusalem for Jesus' dedication. It would be exciting to go to the Temple for the rites of purification and sacrifice. There, Jesus, as firstborn son, would be presented before God in accordance with the Law. They did this, she knew, in memory of the time when God spared the firstborn Israelites when He brought them up out of Egypt. Mary reflected on the wonderful story of the Exodus of her ancestors. Passover would hold new meaning for her this year now that she had a firstborn son, too.

The Law also required that Mary give a sacrifice for her purification. Joseph would buy the sacrifice at the courtyard of the Temple. She wished they could afford a lamb, but they were much too poor for that and would have to settle for a couple of pigeons. Even the birds and the five shekels he would have to pay to redeem his firstborn son would be hard enough to come by. Mary's heart again gave thanks for the Lord's provision of the temporary carpenter shop. Yes, God always met their needs.

The Temple was magnificent! Mary was dazzled by all the sights and sounds at the immense structure of white limestone with its golden gates, colonnades of marble, and richly colored tapestries. It was teeming with priests, musicians, and worshippers.

Much to her astonishment, a venerable old man came directly up to them and reached out to take the baby from her arms. She was so caught off guard that she released the child into his outstretched arms before she even realized what she was doing. They stood amazed as he told them that his name was Simeon and he explained to them that the Holy Spirit had assured him that he would not die until he had seen the Messiah. Blessing God, he prayed and praised God before them, speaking of Jesus as the prophet had told of the Messiah, *"A light for revelation to the Gentiles and for glory to your people Israel."* Joseph and Mary were speechless.

Simeon spoke of the mighty power of the Christ. Then he blessed them but told Mary that she would also suffer deep anguish as well.

As soon as Simeon had finished, an aged prophetess joined them. She also gave thanks to God and spoke about how the child would be the Redeemer. It was all too unexpected and too much to comprehend. They stood there not saying a word.

They eventually headed back to Bethlehem, marveling at all that had taken place. Once again, they discussed the unfathomable responsibility that lay ahead of them of parenting this child. Finally, they were free to consummate their marriage. Thus, another dimension was added to their bonds of love and unity and they praised God together for His goodness.

*****

"Samuel told me today that his uncle's injuries are nearly healed. Do you think that means we will be able to go back home soon?" Mary asked Joseph wistfully as they shared their evening meal. "I am so homesick! Now that Jesus is here, surely our families and friends will all love him. He's such a precious child!" and she looked lovingly at her little son.

"I don't know, Mary," he replied thoughtfully, "I certainly miss my own shop and long to be there, too. I just don't feel that God has released us from this place, yet. But I have no idea why."

Mary sighed. How often had they had this conversation lately? Why didn't Joseph understand how much she needed her mother and family now? It was hard being a young new mother and being alone. There were so many things she didn't know. The neighbors here still saw them as outsiders. She heard the whispers of the women when she went to the well. Instead of accepting them because of what the shepherds had said, the women of the town just stared at her and her son as if they were something strange. She didn't understand why it had to be that way. Sometimes it seemed so unfair. She wanted to go home.

"Help me, Lord God," she prayed silently. "Help me to understand the place you have for me so that I can do Your will."

At that moment they both noticed unusual sounds coming from the street. Joseph got up quickly and went into the shop to see if there were customers looking for him. Mary heard him speaking with some men with a foreign accent, but she couldn't make out what they were saying. Curious, she picked up Jesus and stepped towards the door.

Much to her astonishment she saw that Joseph was leading the way back into their tiny room. She had never laid eyes on anyone like these men before! Her jaw dropped in amazement and she backed against the far wall, clutching Jesus tightly.

"Mary!" Joseph exclaimed his voice full of excitement, "These Magi have been looking for Jesus. They have been traveling to see him ever since the night he was born!" Mary tried not to stare at the elegant clothing and carefully braided beards of the sages who now filled the room. Even the color of their skin was different, she observed. She stood dumbstruck as they, too, prostrated themselves before him and worshipped Jesus just as the shepherds had. Her eyes widened as they solemnly presented him with extravagant gifts of gold and expensive spices.

They told Joseph about their journey and the strange light that had led them to their destination. Then they left as quickly as they had come.

Mary would never forget the look of joy and adoration on those strange Gentile faces. What did it all mean? It was more than Mary could comprehend.

She just sat without moving and held Jesus for a long time after they had left, inhaling the exotic smells left by the perfume of their extraordinary visitors.

"Joseph, look at these gifts the Magi brought! Whatever will we do with them?" Mary greeted Joseph as he returned from the shop.

"They are for Jesus," he reminded her. "If God has provided them, He will also show us what He wants us to do with them." He was as excited and confused as Mary, but in his heart, he knew that he must wait for God's direction.

"What do you suppose they meant about the strange phenomenon they saw in the heavens that told them that the King of the Jews had been born? What ancient writings were they talking about? Do you suppose it was something from the prophet Daniel? Didn't he live in the East?"

Mary laughed as she pictured their visitors asking Herod the Great about where to find her son, the King of the Jews! But Joseph sobered at the thought. He tried not to let Mary see the fear that came over him. Herod was an Idumean that had no legal right to rule over the Jews. Even if Rome thought otherwise, Herod knew better. If this proud and cruel king had killed members of his own family - his own wife and sons - to maintain his power, what might he do to a child whom he perceived to be a Jewish contender to his throne? But this had not occurred to Mary and she continued chattering on about the unbelievable visitors.

"Did you see the beautiful silk robes they all wore? Didn't you think their fancy beards were outrageous?

They were Gentiles, Joseph! Can you imagine that? Worshipping Jesus! Joseph, do you recall what Simeon told us? That Jesus would be a light to the Gentiles. What can it all mean? How can we know how to parent such a child? My mind can't even hold the magnitude of such a thought." And they prayed together for God's wisdom and guidance.

*****

Joseph awoke with a start! It had happened again! A dream!

He looked down at his wife and son sleeping so peacefully. He felt himself nearly bursting with a desire to protect them from all harm. Whatever he must do, he would. He felt joy in the realization that God would entrust the care of two such precious ones to him. He would depend on God and obey no matter what was asked of him.

"Thank You Lord God, for direction," he breathed as he cautiously eased himself to his feet, careful not to waken Mary.

He would get everything ready for them to leave while she slept. His eyes fell on the wonderful gifts the Magi had so reverently placed before the Child. Now he knew what they were for. With these gifts he would be able to provide for his little family as they made their journey into Egypt and stayed there until it would be safe to return home.

As he had become accustomed to doing, his thoughts turned to God and his favorite psalm penetrated his consciousness once again. As he prepared for their hasty departure, he prayed the words of the prayer of his famous ancestor:

Grant your strength to your servant
and save the son of your maidservant.

When all was ready, he gently woke Mary and told her what the angel had said. Sleepy and bewildered, she got up and obediently readied her sleeping son. Without a backward glance, they slipped out of the darkened city and began their long journey to the foreign land.

One thing was very clear to the determined couple as they set out on their journey into unknown territory. They would lay aside all their own expectations for what parenting the Son of God might mean and learn to continually trust God and obey Him without hesitation.

As they moved carefully through the darkness, they drew strength and courage from repeating the words of David's psalm together:

Hear, O Lord, and answer me for I am poor and needy.

Guard my life, for I am devoted to you.

You are my God; save your servant who trusts in you.

Have mercy on me, O Lord, for I call to you all day long.

Bring joy to your servant, for to you O Lord I lift up my soul.

You are forgiving and good, O Lord, abounding in love to all who call to you. Hear my prayer, O Lord;

Listen to my cry for mercy.

In the day of my trouble I will call to you for you will answer me. Among the gods there is none like you O Lord; No deeds can compare with yours.

All the nations you have made will come and worship before you O Lord; They will bring glory to your name.

For you are great and do marvelous deeds; You alone are God.

Teach me your way, O Lord, and I will walk in your truth; Give me an undivided heart, that I may fear your name.

I will praise you, O Lord my God, with all my heart;

I will glorify your name forever,

For great is your love toward me;

You have delivered me from the grave.

The arrogant are attacking me, O God; a band of ruthless men seeks my life – men without regard for you.

But you, O Lord, are a compassionate and gracious God, slow to anger, abounding in love and faithfulness.

Turn to me and have mercy on me;

Grant your strength to your servant and save the son of your maidservant.

Give me a sign of your goodness, that my enemies may see it and be put to shame, for you O Lord, have helped and comforted me.

MOVING FORWARD

Here are some questions to consider for discussion:

- What emotions did you experience as you read this story?
- How are you like Mary (or Joseph) ? How are you different?
- What are some of the ways that you have pictured these events differently than the author imagined them?
- Do you think Zechariah was deaf or only mute? What can you find in scripture to support your conclusion?
- What other details would you changed if you were writing this story.
- Has anything changed in your perspective about Mary and Joseph?
- How has this story impacted your thinking about how we live out our own stories??
- What expectations do you have that might be different than God's plans and purposes for your life?
- How can you use the godly parents of Jesus as examples to follow in your own life?

Look for the CAMPANION JOURNAL TO THIS BOOK CALLED **MY STORY** designed for you to write your thoughts about how God is working in your own life.

Available on Amazon ASIN: BO8KR9B2NV

Here is a fun quiz for you:

CHRISTMAS FACT OR FICTION

What does the BIBLE tell us about Christ's birth? It is fun to use our imagination to try to fill in the details of the Christmas story, but it is important to be able to recognize the difference between Fact and FICTION. Many things that we associate with the Christmas story come from tradition or paintings. Do you know what the scriptures actually tell us?

Mary and Joseph traveled to Bethlehem by

A. Camel

B. Donkey

C. Donkey Cart

D. By Foot

E. Unknown

2. A manger is a

A. Shelter for domestic animals

B. Wooden storage bin

C. Feeding trough

D. None of these

3. According to Scripture which animals were present at the birth of Jesus?

____

4. Who saw the "Star in the East?"

A. Magi

B. Mary & Joseph

C. Shepherds

D. A&C

E, None of these

5. What "sign" were the shepherds told to look for?

. A flashing arrow pointing to the stable.

B. A star

C. A baby that never cries.

D. A baby in a manger

E. A house with a Christmas tree and Santa out front.

F. B&D

G. None of the above

6. There was probably snow that first Christmas

A. Only in the snow belt in Ohio

B. All over Israel

C. Nowhere in Israel

D. Somewhere in Israel

E. Mary and Joseph only dreamed of a white Christmas

6. The baby Jesus cried

A. When the little drummer boy banged on his drum and startled Him

B. Never

C. Just like other babies

7. What is frankincense?

A. A precious metal

B. A precious fabric

C. A precious perfume (incense)

D. A monster movie

F. None of the above

8. According to Matthew, the Magi found Jesus in a

A.Stable

B. House

C. Holiday Inn

D. Palace

F. Matthew did not tell us

9. Myrrh was used as a(n)

A . perfume

B. embalming substance

C. oil for beauty treatments

C. A&B

D. A, B&C

E. None of the above

9. How many "wise men" came to Jesus?

A. Three

B. Unknown

C. Four

10. Which statement is untrue? The wise men [Magi] were probably

A. from Persia (now the area of Iran)

B. kings

C. astrologers

D. wealthy

E. visiting Jesus as a toddler

11. Circle all the correct responses: The story of the birth of Jesus can be found in

A. Matthew

B. Mark

C. Luke

D. John

Correct responses: 1. E; 2. C; 3. None (Scripture doesn't list any animals) 4. A; 5. D; 6. D; 7. C; 8. C; 9. B; 10. E; 11. E; 12.B All true except kings. They probably held no governmental position. 13. Matthew, Luke

Do you agree with these conclusions?

ABOUT THE AUTHORS

Baker Family Ministries is a collaborative effort of a family who wants to share the Good News of Jesus Christ with you and your family. Although we are the Baker Family, we are not bakers, but (as the old saying goes); see ourselves more as beggars who want to show others where we have found bread.

This Christmas story is written by Hazel Partington (better known as Mama in our family), and edited by her son-in-law, Jody Baker.

Rev. Dr. Hazel Partington has joyfully served the Lord for nearly 5 decades of ministry. Hazel and her husband of over 55 years have numerous grandchildren from their many children (by birth, adoption, foster care, and others who have found a home with them at critical times in their lives.)

Rev. Jody Baker is an upcoming author whose purpose is to help his readers draw into a deeper relationship with Jesus. He currently serves as pastor of Wildare United Methodist Church in Cortland, Ohio, USA. He is blessed to be married to Patti and loves spending time with their three children: Sage, PJ, and Wesley.

From The Baker Family:

3 WAYS TO HELP YOU FORGIVE:

FORGIVENESS ISN'T EASY: But It Is the Key to Forgiveness ISBN: 979-8-6978-1610-3

GOING DEEPER WHEN FORGIVNESS ISN'T EASY: An Interactive Workbook for Individual or Small-Group Study ISBN:13- 979-8-5539-1692-3

FORGIVENESS JOURNAL: A Lined Notebook for Recording Your Healing and Personal Growth
ISBN: 979-8-6977-3182-6

His and Her journals with simple thought-provoking prompts to help you express your thoughts to God.

ISBN:13- 979-8-5560-0817-5

ISBN:13-979-8-5544-6518-5

LOOK FOR THEM ON AMAZON.

More Lined Journals from the Baker Family

ISBN:13- 979-8-5504-4432-0 ISBN: 13-979-8-5545-2250-

Use your creativity to explore your own thoughts and reflections in these blank lined journals.

ISBN:13- 979 8-6904-4286-6

Made in the USA
Monee, IL
13 December 2020